LUCY'S WISH

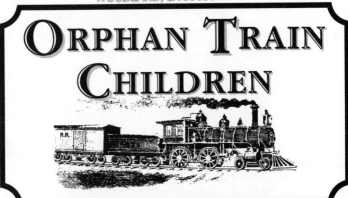

ORPHAN TRAIN CHILDREN

LUCY'S WISH

Joan Lowery Nixon

DELACORTE PRESS

*With thanks to Amy Berkower and Dan Weiss,
who envisioned the orphan train stories.*

PUBLISHED BY DELACORTE PRESS
Bantam Doubleday Dell Publishing Group, Inc.
1540 Broadway
New York, New York 10036

Text copyright © 1998 by Joan Lowery Nixon
and Daniel Weiss Associates, Inc.

Jacket illustration copyright © 1998 by Lori Earley

Library of Congress Cataloging-in-Publication Data
Nixon, Joan Lowery.
Lucy's wish / Joan Lowery Nixon.
p. cm. — (Orphan train children ; #1)
Summary: Ten-year-old Lucy, an orphan who wants a little sister more than anything, finds a very special one in the less than perfect family which she joins.
ISBN 0-385-32293-3
[1. Orphans—Fiction. 2. Sisters—Fiction. 3. Orphan trains—Fiction.] I. Title. II. Series: Nixon, Joan Lowery. Orphan train children ; #1.
PZ7.N65Lu 1998   97-21529
[Fic]—dc21   CIP
                                                               AC

The text of this book is set in 13-point Adobe Garamond.
Book design by Susan Clark

Manufactured in the United States of America
March 1998
BVG   10   9   8   7   6   5   4   3   2

A Note from the Author

In the 1850s there were many homeless children in New York City. The Children's Aid Society, which was founded by Charles Loring Brace, tried to help these children by giving them new homes. They were sent west and placed with families who lived on farms and in small towns throughout the United States. From 1854 to 1929, groups of homeless children traveled on trains that were soon nicknamed orphan trains. The children were called orphan train riders.

The characters in these stories are fictional, but their problems and joys, their worries and fears, and their desire to love and be loved were experienced by the real orphan train riders of many years ago.

Joan Lowery Nixon

More orphan train stories by
Joan Lowery Nixon

A FAMILY APART
Winner of the Golden Spur Award
CAUGHT IN THE ACT
IN THE FACE OF DANGER
Winner of the Golden Spur Award
A PLACE TO BELONG
A DANGEROUS PROMISE
KEEPING SECRETS
CIRCLE OF LOVE

LUCY'S WISH
WILL'S CHOICE

Homes Wanted
For Children

A Company of Orphan Children

of different ages in charge of an agent will arrive at your town on date herein mentioned. The object of the coming of these children is to find homes in your midst, especially among farmers, where they may enjoy a happy and wholesome family life, where kind care, good example and moral training will fit them for a life of self-support and usefulness. They come under the auspices of the New York Children's Aid Society. They have been tested and found to be well-meaning boys and girls anxious for homes.

The conditions are that these children shall be properly clothed, treated as members of the family, given proper school advantages and remain in the family until they are eighteen years of age. At the expiration of the time specified it is hoped that arrangements can be made whereby they may be able to remain in the family indefinitely. The Society retains the right to remove a child at any time for just cause, and agrees to remove any found unsatisfactory after being notified.

Remember the time and place. All are invited. Come out and hear the address. Applications may be made to any one of the following well known citizens, who have agreed to act as local committee to aid the agent in securing homes.

A. J. Hammond,   H. W. Parker,   Geo. Baxter,   J. F. Damon,   J. P. Humes,
H. N. Welch,   J. A. Armstrong,   F. L. Durgin.

This distribution of Children is by Consent of the State Board of Control, and will take place at the

G. A. R. Hall, Winnebago, Minn.
Friday, Jan. 11th, '07, at 10.30 a. m. @ 2 p. m.

H. D. Clarke, State Agent,
Dodge Center, Minn.

Office: 105 East 22nd St.,
New York City.

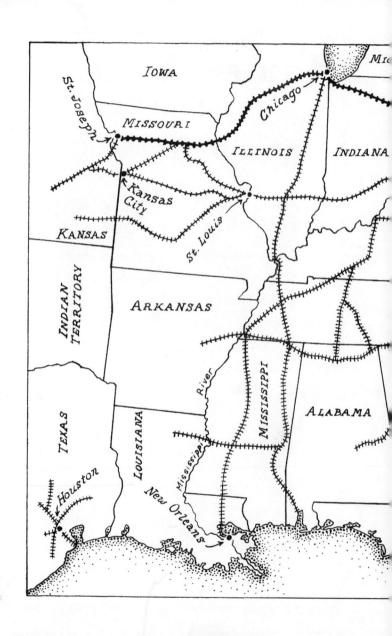

From the journal of
FRANCES MARY KELLY, JULY 1866

Our orphan train is on its way to Missouri. I hope with all my heart that the children in my care will be placed out with loving foster parents.

The children try to be brave. But I can see the fear in their eyes: Will I be chosen? Will anyone want me?

Some of the children want only to be comforted, but others ask for promises they must know I can't make. Today ten-year-old Lucy Griggs tugged at my skirt. Her shy smile and pleading gaze touched my heart.

"Will you help me find a family?" she asked.

"Of course," I told her.

"I want a special family," Lucy said. "I want a mother and a father and a little sister for me to love. I've always wanted to have a little sister."

My heart ached for Lucy. When she was six, soon after coming to the United States from England, her father was killed in an accident. When her mother

1

died a few weeks ago, Lucy was evicted from the one-room apartment she had shared with her mother. Lucy had no one to care for her until she was rescued by the Children's Aid Society.

I tried to help her face the truth. "Lucy, dear," I said, "if people already have one child, they may not have enough money to take care of another child."

But Lucy's eyes shone. "Oh, yes, they will! You see, their little girl will want a big sister. She'll be looking for me." She held out the doll she calls "Baby" and said, "I'm going to share Baby with my little sister."

I hugged Lucy, unable to answer. Please let it be so *were the only words that came to my mind, for I have no way of knowing what will happen to Lucy.*

CHAPTER ONE

Lucy Amanda Griggs squirmed between the two large boxes she had found in the alley. Even though she was very tired, she couldn't sleep. The ground was hard and lumpy, and the bright morning sunlight forced Lucy to open her eyes.

She tugged her ragged shawl up to cover her head. Her hair felt damp and greasy. How long had it been since she'd had a bath? Lucy couldn't remember.

She smiled at Baby, cradling the doll in her arms. One side of Baby's face was covered with a spiderweb of cracks. And there was a hole in her cloth body, where Lucy had to keep poking the stuffing back inside. Lucy didn't care. She had found Baby in a trash bin. She knew that Baby needed her, and she needed Baby. The cracks, the faded dress, and the hole didn't matter. From the moment Lucy saw Baby she loved her.

Lucy rocked Baby and sang to her. It was a soft, sleepy song that Lucy's mother had always sung to her. "Rock, rock, my baby-o. Rock, rock, my baby."

But Lucy's song melted into tears as memories of her mother swept over her.

She angrily brushed the tears away. Crying didn't help. Lucy remembered the time when Mum had told her that Father had been killed in an accident. It was four years ago. Lucy and Mum had clung to each other and sobbed, but their tears hadn't brought Father back.

Lucy shivered and hugged Baby tightly. She thought about the terrible day when Mum had died of cholera. That was four—or was it five?—weeks ago. Inspectors from the Metropolitan Board of Health had hurried into Lucy and Mum's room. The inspectors were afraid that the disease would spread. Cholera had already killed more than two thousand New Yorkers. Even before the inspectors left, the landlord, Mr. Beam, had ordered Lucy to leave the building.

He had clutched her shoulder as he pushed her toward the doorway. "It's a matter of business. I've got to clean up that room and rent it to someone who can pay," he'd said. His eyes were not on Lucy, but on the inspectors.

Lucy had been so frightened that her heart had pounded. She'd clenched her hands to keep them from shaking. "But, sir, I've got nowhere to go," she had pleaded.

Mr. Beam had glanced nervously at the inspectors. He had lowered his voice and answered, "I can't worry about your problems. I've got enough of my own. The Board of Health like to have ruined me last February.

They blame the landlords for the cholera that swept through this city."

He had cleared his throat with an angry *ha-rumph!* and added, "Meeting their demands to clean up and make repairs cost me a great deal of money. I've nothing to spare, so don't be coming to me for help."

Weak from fear, but with no choice, Lucy had wandered out to the street. She had plopped down on a curb, heedless of the hooves of the horses and the heavy wagon wheels that rumbled near her toes. She had wept in sorrow, but her tears hadn't brought Mum back. They hadn't helped at all.

As Lucy's sobs became dry shudders, she had looked up and seen the Olneys' butcher shop across the street.

Sometimes Mum, with Lucy in hand, had stopped by the shop. Sometimes she had managed to come up with enough coins to buy a small piece of meat or a soup bone. And sometimes

Mum had played with and talked to the Olneys' son, Henry.

Mrs. Olney looked unhappy whenever anyone asked her about Henry. "Never been right in the head since he was born," she said. "Can't nothin' be done about it."

Mum had treated Henry the way she treated everybody else. Henry tried to talk to Mum, and Mum seemed to understand. When she paid attention to Henry, he smiled and laughed.

Once Lucy overheard another neighbor say, "I'm always kind to the lad. I tell myself, 'There but for the grace of God go I.'"

Under her breath, so that only Lucy could hear, Mum had whispered, "I tell myself, 'There go I.'"

Later, when they were alone, Lucy had asked Mum, "Why is Mrs. Olney always so cross? Why doesn't she ever talk to Henry?"

Mum had shaken her head sadly. "Mrs. Olney wanted a strong, healthy child who could work in the shop and learn his father's trade. She's so bitter, she can't see that Henry has feelings like everyone else."

Lucy thought about the blue-and-green marble Mum had found and had given to Henry. He had laughed and clapped his hands with joy. "You know what Henry likes, and you can talk with him," Lucy had said. "I wish Mrs. Olney would try."

"Maybe someday she will," Mum had said. "For now, you and I will be Henry's friends."

Lucy shook away the memories and slowly got up from the curb. She crossed the street, darting between the carts and wagons, and entered the butcher shop.

Mr. Olney was not in sight. Mrs. Olney stood behind the counter. Gruffly she said, "G'dafternoon, Lucy. Sorry to hear about your ma. She was a good woman."

Lucy nodded, too frightened to speak.

"Well, what's done is done. That's the way of

life. So let's get on with it," Mrs. Olney said. "Did you come to buy a small chop? A pat of ground beef?"

Trying not to look at the blood-soaked wooden chopping block, Lucy spoke up. "I have no money to buy food, and I have nowhere to live. I've come for a job. I'll sweep. I'll scrub. I'm ten years old—big enough to do hard work."

Mrs. Olney's lips turned down, and she gave a loud sniff. "You're just a slip of a girl, Lucy Griggs. You're scarcely big enough to lift and carry a bucket of water. But if it's hard work you want, I've got plenty of that for you. In turn, you'll get two meals a day and a pallet to put down by the fire."

"Thank you," Lucy whispered.

Hot tears rushed to her eyes, but Mrs. Olney snapped at her. "No time to waste on tears. Understand? Get a scrub brush, a large rag, and a bucket from the back room. Those Board of

Health inspectors might poke their noses round here, so the floor and walls will need to be scrubbed down."

Henry followed Lucy. As she bent to pick up a bucket, he reached out and gently touched her tear-damp face. Lucy couldn't tell what he said, but she heard the question in his voice.

"I'm sad, Henry," she told him. "I've lost my mum and I miss her. I'm sad."

Henry seemed to understand. His face looked sad, too. But in an instant he brightened. He pulled the shiny blue-and-green marble from his pocket and pressed it into Lucy's hand.

Lucy tried to give it back. "Mum gave this to you," she said.

Henry smiled and nodded as he backed off, his hands behind him.

"You really want me to have this," Lucy said, surprised at the joy in Henry's eyes. "Thank you, Henry. It's a beautiful gift. I'll keep it forever."

"Where are you, girl?" Mrs. Olney's voice was sharp.

Lucy quickly tucked the marble into her pocket, picked up the bucket and rags, and ran to fill the bucket.

Lucy worked hard each day from well before light until late at night. But, remembering what Mum had said, she always found time to talk to Henry. She could understand some of Henry's speech. She could make him smile. Sometimes, together, they played with the marble.

Then one morning Lucy awoke ill and feverish. Everything went wrong that day. She spilled a pitcher of milk, and then dropped and chipped Mrs. Olney's heavy china platter.

"You'll have to go," Mrs. Olney grumbled. "I can't waste any more time coddling the likes of you. One problem child's enough to care for."

Shaken, Lucy begged, "Could I say good-bye to Henry?"

"As if he'd understand!" Mrs. Olney snapped. "Can't you see how busy I am? The last thing I need right now is the two of you underfoot. Get your things and go!"

Lucy ran, clutching the marble in her pocket. *I won't forget you, Henry,* she promised.

In her shelter Lucy shuddered at the unhappy memory. She held Baby even more tightly.

She was startled when a low voice outside broke into her thoughts. "Lucy! Hsst! Lucy!"

CHAPTER TWO

Lucy recognized the voice, so she pushed aside one of the boxes. Her friend Joey, a wiry, dark-haired boy, smiled at her. "Good. You're still here," he said.

Lucy smiled in return. "Thank you for helping me last night," she said. "When Mrs. Olney threw me out, I didn't know where to go."

"Lots of kids sleep in alleys," Joey answered. "It's just lucky I knew about this place and got you here before anybody else found it." He crawled into her shelter. "Feeling better?" he asked.

Lucy nodded. "The apple and bread you gave me must have helped."

"So you're not hungry anymore?"

Lucy's stomach gave a hollow rumble. Both she and Joey burst out laughing.

He reached inside his ragged jacket, pulled out a banana, and held it out to Lucy.

Lucy knew that Joey had no money to buy such a treat. She suspected that the banana had disappeared from a peddler's cart. But she was too hungry to ask questions. She grabbed the banana and gulped it down.

Joey's eyes twinkled with mischief. "If you could make a wish, what would it be? A full stomach? A clean bed in a real house?"

Lucy surprised even herself as she said, "I'd wish for someone to love me."

Joey blinked and smiled sadly. "I can't give you that wish, but I can give you the next best thing." He tugged a scrap of paper from his pocket.

"One of my chums who lives in the tenements got a letter," he said. "It's from a lad name of

Bertie Jarvis. He used to be one of us, living on the street. Then he went west on an orphan train."

"What's an orphan train?" Lucy asked.

"They're trains that take kids who live on the streets to homes on farms out west. Now, listen. I'm not good at reading, so I was careful to remember the words. The lad wrote that the people who took him in were treating him swell. He said, 'Tell the others. Come west on the orphan trains. Get a new mother and father. It's a good life.'"

Lucy's heart leapt. A new mother and father? For an instant she could feel the warmth of her own mother's arms around her. No other woman could ever replace Mum. But if the new mother was part of a family . . . a family with a little sister for her . . . "Are *you* going west?" Lucy asked.

"What? Go to some strange place I never heard tell of? Not me," Joey answered.

"But a mother and a father . . ."

"Who needs a mother and father?" Joey asked.

"I like New York City. I'm free here to do whatever I like. I don't want to go nowhere else—especially to a farm where I'd have to work." He made a face. "Feed the pigs. That's what they'd have me do. Feed the pigs, and that's not for me."

"I want a mother and father," Lucy said. "And a little sister. They could make my wish come true." She rubbed her nose hard so tears wouldn't come. "How can I find out about the orphan trains?"

Joey grinned and handed her a scrap of paper. "I got my chum to write down the address of the Children's Aid Society. The people there send orphans to homes in the West."

Thankful that Mum had taught her to read, Lucy studied the address.

"I know where the offices are, and I'll take you part of the way," Joey said. "But after that you'll have to find your way to the Society's offices by yourself. I got myself in a bit of trouble with an officer on that beat, so it's best I not show my face around there for a while."

Lucy scrambled out of the shelter and stood up. The hot sun beat against her back. "That means I won't be seeing you again," she said.

For a moment Joey looked so lonely that Lucy wished she could hug him. But Joey wouldn't know what to do with a hug.

"I hope," he said in a rush of words, "I hope you get your wish, Lucy."

"Thank you," Lucy said. "But don't tell it to anyone. Wishes are supposed to be kept secret."

"Then it's my secret, too," Joey said. He gently punched her shoulder and gave her a smile.

"Joey . . . ," Lucy began. She wondered how she could find the words to thank him for all that he'd done to help. But before she could, Joey turned to leave. "C'mon, Lucy. We ought to get moving."

Lucy smoothed her hair from her eyes, wrapped Baby snugly into her shawl, and followed Joey in the direction of the Children's Aid Society.

CHAPTER THREE

Lucy nervously entered the Children's Aid Society offices. A plump woman with a soft, kind face hurried toward her.

Lucy took a deep breath and let her words tumble out. "My name is Lucy Amanda Griggs. I need help. My father died when I was six, and now my mother is dead. I want to go west on an orphan train to find a new mother and father and a little sister."

She stopped and took another gulp of air. Then she added, "And I'm hungry."

The woman knelt before Lucy. "My name is Miss Hunter," she said. "The first thing we need to do is feed you, and then we'll give you a hot bath and some clean clothing."

She reached for Lucy's doll, but Lucy held tight. "You can't have Baby. I'm the only one who takes care of her."

"That's fine, dear," Miss Hunter said. "Although I do think Baby would like to have her dress washed and ironed."

Lucy thought a moment, then handed Baby to Miss Hunter. "Baby has a hole in her side. Her stuffing keeps coming out."

"I'm very good at mending holes," Miss Hunter told her. "You and Baby will soon feel much better."

"When I get a little sister I'm going to share Baby with her," Lucy said. Miss Hunter's eyes grew wide, but Lucy continued. "I'll have a mother and father and a little sister." Her wish would come true. It had to.

Lucy was fed a meal of soup and bread, and even had a hot bath. Miss Hunter gave her a pretty blue cotton dress, underpants, a camisole and petticoat, nightgown, stockings, and shoes with just a little extra room to grow into.

Lucy looked in the mirror and thought, *Oh, Mum, I wish you could see this lovely dress.*

Miss Dolan, a thin, tired-looking woman, sat Lucy down in a tiny cubbyhole office. She told Lucy the Society's rules for families who agreed to take in orphan train children. "The children are to be treated like one of the family. They will do chores, just as any children in a family would do. They will have good food, fresh air, and sunshine. They will be taken to church on Sundays and be schooled until the age of fourteen."

Miss Dolan didn't smile as she added, "There will be thirty children in your group. I will be your escort on the train to Missouri. I expect all the children in my care to be quiet and well-behaved. I do not allow excess noise, running up and down the aisle, or leaning out the train windows. Is that clearly understood?"

Lucy nodded.

"Do you have any questions?"

Lucy tried hard not to think of her own mother, because when she did tears flooded her eyes. "I . . . I don't know this place called Missouri. I don't know what it's like. Is . . . is this where I'll find a new mother and father and a little sister?"

Miss Dolan sighed and pressed one hand to her side as if it hurt. "My dear child, there is no way we can promise that you'll have a little sister. We're thankful enough when we're able to place each child. We carefully try to screen each family who applies. Most of the people who have taken in our children have been generous and kind."

Most? Lucy thought. *Why didn't she say "all of the people"? What was wrong with the rest of them?* She was afraid to ask.

Over the next few days Lucy met some of the other children with whom she'd be going west. She clung to Baby, who'd been cleaned and mended, and to her wish. Again and again she said to herself, *I want someone to love me. I want*

someone to love me. And, no matter what Miss Do-
lan said, I am going to have a little sister.

One day Lucy heard that the pain in Miss Dolan's side had grown worse. She had been taken to the hospital. Frances Mary Kelly, a pretty young woman with dark hair and smiling eyes, took her place. Miss Kelly would be the one to care for the orphan train riders traveling to Missouri.

As the children were introduced to Miss Kelly, Lucy held up her doll. "This is Baby," she said. "I found her in a trash can, and now she's mine."

"She's lovely, Lucy," Miss Kelly said. She smiled at Baby before she turned to the next child in line.

A girl with flyaway golden hair reached out to stroke Baby's head. "You've got a doll—a real doll," she said. "I had a doll once. I had almost one hundred dolls."

"One hundred?" Lucy gasped. "Nobody has one hundred dolls."

"I did . . . when I was a princess."

Lucy took a careful look at the golden-haired girl. She was taller than Lucy, but she looked close to Lucy's age. "What's your name?" Lucy asked.

"Virginia Hooper. But that's not my real name. My real name is Princess."

"If you're really a princess," Lucy asked, "then why don't you live in a palace? And why is your name Virginia Hooper?"

Virginia looked sad. "Because somebody took me away from my palace when I was very, very young. But I remember. I remember everything."

Lucy didn't believe Virginia. But before she could say so, a girl with freckles and light brown pigtails joined them. "Hello. What's your name?" she asked Lucy.

"Lucy Griggs," Lucy answered. "What's yours?"

Virginia interrupted. "She's Daisy Gordon, and she's only nine."

"Who cares? What's so grand about being

ten?" Daisy answered. As she grinned, crinkling her pug nose, Lucy could see that Daisy was missing two teeth.

Lucy smiled at Daisy. "Maybe my little sister will be like you," she said.

"I'd like to be your little sister," Daisy said.

"You can't be sisters," Virginia insisted.

"Then we'll be friends," Lucy said. She sat down on a nearby bench to show Daisy her doll.

Virginia quickly sat with them. "I don't have any friends," she said.

Lucy wanted to tell snobby Virginia she didn't care, but she remembered how Mum was always kind to everyone. She swallowed the words that wanted to come out and said, "Daisy and I are your friends."

Virginia studied Lucy for a moment, then nodded. "We can only be friends until we're placed out. Then we'll never see each other again."

Daisy took Lucy's hand and gripped it tightly. "Maybe not. Maybe we'll be neighbors," she said.

"I suppose," Virginia said. She slid closer to Lucy. "I've been thinking, what if we're not placed out? What if no one wants us? I heard that children who aren't chosen are sold to peddlers."

Lucy gasped. "Who told you that?"

Virginia pointed at a boy who was a head taller than the other boys with him. "Marcus Melo. He's twelve. He knows a lot of things. He said that one of the orphans ran off into Indian country and was never heard of again."

Daisy shuddered and clung to Lucy even more tightly. Lucy wanted to comfort her, but fear was like a cold finger that wiggled up her backbone. For a moment Lucy was too frightened to remember her wish.

CHAPTER FOUR

The whispered stories grew even more frightening as the orphans got ready for their journey.

"The United States government is building forts across the Indian Territory from North Dakota down to Texas," Marcus said. He brushed a strand of dark hair from his eyes. "I read it in a newspaper."

"What are forts? Why is the government building them?" Virginia asked.

Marcus smiled as if he knew everything. "Every day the Comanches and Arapahoes—the best of

City and the boats that sailed along the Hudson River. She wanted to remember them forever, as she would her mother and father. She'd never see her parents again. She'd never see the city again. She touched the marble in her pocket. Did Henry wonder where she had gone? Did he miss her? Lucy tried hard to keep the tears from spilling down her cheeks, but she couldn't.

Beside her, Daisy sniffled. Lucy put an arm around her. Other children in the wagon were crying, too.

As much as Lucy wanted a new family, it was scary to begin the journey to find one. Were the people in Missouri like the people in New York City? Did they have enough to eat?

Miss Kelly had told the children that many of them would be living on farms. But what did farms look like? How were they different from the one room Lucy and her parents had lived in? She wondered where the fruit and vegetables grew. In big boxes? Or on trees? Maybe there would be an

all the Indian fighters—ride out of the hills to attack. Our Sixth Cavalry has to fight back. There are terrible battles." He put his hands around his throat and made a choking noise.

Lucy gasped. "There aren't any Indians where we're going, are there?"

"Probably lots of them," Marcus's friend Sam said in a low, scary voice. "They're likely to snatch you up and carry you away if they get a chance."

Finally Lucy couldn't stand hearing one more tale. She saw Miss Hunter whisk past, and she followed her into her office.

Lucy kept a firm grip on Baby as she asked, "Is it true that orphans are sometimes carried off by Indians? Or that we'll have to live in the barn with the animals and eat only the slops left by the pigs?"

Miss Hunter gasped. "Of course not! Where did you hear a dreadful story like that?"

Lucy continued, a little more bravely. "Do orphan girls have to sit in a small room sewing all day and all night until their fingers bleed and their eyes fall out?"

Miss Hunter knelt and held Lucy's shoulders, looking into her eyes. "Oh, dear me," she said. "These stories aren't true. You'll all be placed out with people who are approved by a committee of the town leaders. The people who come to see the orphan train riders *want* to have a child in the family. Maybe they've always wanted to have a child but couldn't. Or maybe their children have died. We'll do our best to find happy homes for you. I promise."

Lucy's relief was so great that she threw her arms around Miss Hunter's neck.

Miss Hunter hugged her back. Then she said, "If all the children have heard these stories, it's time I put an end to them."

Miss Hunter called all thirty children together and told them again about the placing-out system. She explained why the rumors they'd heard couldn't possibly be true.

"One of our agents will visit you about six months after you've been placed," Miss Hunter said. "He'll talk to you and make sure that you and your foster parents are happy. If you're not he'll find a new home for you. We will do our very best to see that you have homes with good people who will take care of you."

Lucy smiled to herself. Now she was sure that her wish was going to come true.

Before the group of children was taken to train, each child was given a parcel. It held change of clothing, a comb, and a toothbrush.

Lucy held her parcel carefully, balancing it Baby. She climbed into one of the three wa that would take them to the train station.

Daisy and Virginia crowded in beside Once the wagons were moving, Lucy searche faces of the ragged street children who sta them as they passed. *Joey?* she thought. *Wh you? It's time to say good-bye.*

But there was no sign of Joey.

Lucy studied the tall buildings of Ne

onion-and-potato tree. Maybe she would climb the tree to pick the vegetables for dinner.

Lucy glanced back at the second wagon and saw Miss Kelly perched on the board seat next to the driver. Miss Kelly smiled and waved at Lucy. Lucy waved back.

Daisy gave another sob, and Lucy hugged her. "Everything is going to be all right, Daisy," Lucy told her friend. She began to softly sing, "Rock, rock, my baby-o. Rock, rock, my baby."

"I'm not a baby," Daisy mumbled.

Lucy sighed. She needed a little sister who was young enough to sing to. "I know you're not," she told Daisy. "I was . . . I was singing to my doll."

Daisy raised her head. "Have you ever been on a train, Lucy?"

"No," Lucy said. "But it should be a wonder. Think of all the things we'll see from the windows."

Daisy nodded, but she didn't say anything.

Even Virginia didn't speak. Everyone was silent until the wagons reached the train depot and the children and Miss Kelly scrambled out.

The train was large—much bigger than Lucy had thought it would be. It was like a giant snake that growled and grumbled to itself.

The engine gave a sudden loud snort of steam, and Lucy jumped.

There were people everywhere. The wooden platform next to the train was crowded with them. Lucy felt lost in a swirl of long, dark travel skirts, parasols, uniforms, frock coats, and top hats. She was glad when Miss Kelly patted her shoulder. Miss Kelly lined the children up and led them to the steps of one of the passenger cars.

"Everybody on board!" she cried, checking off names on a paper she carried.

Lucy climbed on board and sat in one of the wooden benchlike seats near the middle of the car. Daisy sat in the same seat next to the window, and Virginia sat on Lucy's other side.

While Daisy stared out the window, Lucy

32

watched two of the older girls settle into seats with their young charges. On this trip, the older girls got to be "big sisters" to the toddlers.

I could be a wonderful big sister, Lucy thought. *I could be the best big sister in the world.* She fought back a shiver of jealousy as she saw two-year-old Lizzie Ann Schultz wrap her arms around pretty Mary Beth Lansdown's neck and plant a kiss on her cheek.

Lucy tried to picture the family who was going to adopt her. *There will be a smiling father and a mother who will hug me. And there will be a little sister who will sit on my lap and say, "I love you, Lucy."*

"All aboard!" the conductor called.

There was a last-minute bustle as people found their seats. The train jerked and rocked as the engine slowly began to chug forward.

Faster and faster the train went, clicking over the tracks. Lucy took a deep breath. Her heart pounded. At last they were on their way. "To find my family," Lucy whispered to herself.

CHAPTER FIVE

The train quickly left behind the cluttered streets and cramped buildings of the city. And soon there were wonderful things to see from the train's wide windows. There were open stretches of land planted with green, growing things. Horses ran from the noisy engine and clattering cars. Cows either gave the train a curious stare or just kept grazing. And there were tidy farmhouses. Real houses! The children crowded to the windows.

"Look at that white house with two chimneys! It's so big. How many families do you think live in that house?" Lucy asked.

"Just one family," a boy named Eddie said. "Those houses are for rich folks."

As they passed a farmhouse, a woman put down the broom she'd been using to sweep her front stoop and waved at the children. Lucy eagerly waved back. Soon she might find herself living in a house like that one. Her new mother would be as friendly as that woman. And inside the house would be a smiling father and, best of all, a little sister.

The days on the train seemed very long, even though Miss Kelly told stories and sang to the children. They ate bread and cheese and apples, which Miss Kelly pulled from a large basket. And they drank fresh milk, which Miss Kelly bought at some of the depots where the train stopped.

But the seats on the train were hard, and the passenger car rocked and wobbled. The worst part was at night, when the lights were turned low. That was when Lucy was the loneliest.

One night a few of the girls who were still

awake whispered about the families who might want them.

"At the orphan asylum we had to work or study every minute," Aggie Vaughn said. "We had just half an hour to go outside. That was the only time we were allowed to talk to each other."

Jessie Kay Lester was shocked. "You could only talk for half an hour a day?"

Virginia giggled. "Can you imagine Jessie not talking all day long?"

Aggie didn't smile. "Maybe the people who take us in will make us work just as hard as they did at the asylum."

There was silence for a moment. Then Daisy said, "They'll be our new parents. We'll have to do whatever they tell us to do."

There was a hard knot in Lucy's stomach. She clung tightly to Baby. Their new parents would be good to them, wouldn't they?

No one had anything else to say. Daisy rested her head on Lucy's shoulder, and Lucy used Baby as a pillow.

I wish for someone to love me. I wish for someone to love me, Lucy repeated until the words slid away into dreams.

The next day was the fourth day of their journey. As soon as everyone had eaten breakfast, Miss Kelly told the children that the train's first stop would be that very day in Harwood, Missouri. Miss Kelly's announcement made Lucy terribly nervous. She tugged at Miss Kelly's skirt and asked, "Will you help me find a family?"

"Of course I will," Miss Kelly said, hugging her tightly. But Lucy knew there wasn't much Miss Kelly could do. Lucy's wish was her only hope. But would wishing over and over again be enough to make it come true?

Before they arrived in Harwood, the train came to a sudden stop. A man jumped from the train, waving a gun. There were men on horseback waiting for him, and they rode away in a hurry.

The man had been in their car, but Lucy had hardly even noticed him. The older boys were excited and talked about Confederate soldiers and robbers and murderers until Lucy became scared all over again. Was this what the West was going to be like?

Miss Kelly soothed the children. "He's gone," she said. "He won't frighten us again."

Lucy relaxed and turned her thoughts to more important things. Soon the train would arrive in Harwood. People would come to see them and choose them. Would her new family be there?

Miss Kelly brushed the girls' hair and tied ribbons into big, white bows. Lucy loved her bow. It was the first one she'd ever had.

Each child was given a clean cotton handkerchief. Lucy shoved hers into her skirt pocket. She was surprised when her fingers touched a cool, smooth, round surface. As she pulled out the marble, she thought, *Henry's gift.* The swirl of blues and greens made her think of Mum and home. Lucy held back her tears.

The train began to slow, and Miss Kelly called out, "Settle down, children. I want you to listen."

Lucy dropped the marble back into her pocket.

Miss Kelly said, "Children, you're going to discover many fine people who want very much to meet you. Some of you will find new families here."

Jessie spoke softly. "What happens if we don't?"

Lucy's heart began to thump hard. Miss Kelly answered, "Then you'll still have me. I'll be with you. I won't leave you until you all find homes."

"Do you promise? You will stay with us?" Lucy asked.

"I promise," Miss Kelly said. "My job is to make sure that you all have good homes."

Lucy's heart grew quiet. But she still held tightly to Baby. She still hoped with all her heart that her wish would come true.

When the train stopped in Harwood, a man came aboard to greet Miss Kelly. She turned to the children and said, "Pick up your luggage, boys and girls. We'll leave the train and walk two blocks to the Methodist church, where we'll meet the people who have come to see you. Remember, you're wonderful children, and I'm very, very proud of you. The families who get you will be lucky, so hold your heads high and smile."

There were a lot of people on the platform who had come just to look at the orphans. Lucy blushed. She hated being stared at. She hated hearing people talk about her as though she couldn't hear. Staring straight ahead, she followed Miss Kelly and the other children down a dusty street to the Methodist church.

The church was filled with people. At one end there was a raised platform. Three rows of stools were on the platform, and Miss Kelly seated the children on the stools. The smallest were in front, the largest in back. Lucy found herself at one end of the middle row.

When they were all settled, Miss Kelly told the people who had come to see the children about the Children's Aid Society. Then she introduced each child.

Lucy was terrified when her name was called.

She looked out at all the faces and wondered whether anyone there would want her. Daisy was introduced next, and all the eyes turned to look at Daisy.

Miss Kelly invited those who had come to visit the stage and get to know the children. A buzz of voices quickly filled the room.

A woman ran to swoop up little Lizzie, and Lucy saw two of the older boys being chosen.

Choose me, she thought, and dared to look into the eyes of a young couple who were standing nearby. But their eyes were on sisters Emily and Harriet Averill. Neither the woman nor the man glanced in Lucy's direction.

Lucy knew she should smile, but she was too frightened. She wrapped her arms around herself, scarcely daring to look up.

Couples strolled nearby. Some of them stopped to chat with one or more of the children. Many of the stools on the platform emptied as people signed the papers to take an orphan train rider.

The room became quieter. Lucy heard Miss Kelly thank the committee members for their help, and she heard someone behind her sob.

She quickly straightened and looked around the room. It was practically empty. Only a few of the orphan train children were left.

"No one chose us," Lucy whispered in surprise and fear. "No one wanted us."

Miss Kelly stepped up to Lucy and took her hand.

"Don't worry," she said. "We have two more stops to make. We will find a family for you."

She smiled, but Lucy didn't smile back. She had never been so scared in her life.

CHAPTER SIX

Lucy counted. At least she wasn't the only one not chosen. Twelve other children stood together. They waited to hear what Miss Kelly would tell them.

Daisy clutched Lucy's arm and whispered, "Virginia got chosen. Why didn't we?"

Lucy didn't answer, but she thought she knew. She had watched Virginia. Virginia had smiled and talked to the people who stopped in front of her.

Miss Kelly had told them that there would be two more stops. Lucy took a deep breath to steady herself. She wouldn't let herself become so scared at the next stop. She'd look at the people who paused to talk to her. She'd do her best to smile.

This time she'd *make* her wish come true.

"We'll catch the midmorning train tomorrow," Miss Kelly said. Then she matched the children with adults who had offered to put them up for the night.

Lucy and Daisy walked with Mrs. Judson, who lived just down the street from the Methodist church. Mrs. Judson didn't say much to them. However, she led Lucy and Daisy into her kitchen and fed them big bowls of tasty mutton stew. When they had eaten all they wanted, Mrs. Judson showed them her guest bedroom, where they'd spend the night.

"There are clean towels by the washbasin and pitcher," she said. "If you need anything else, just call me."

She left the room, closing the door behind her.

Daisy stared openmouthed at the matching pitcher and basin. "Hand-painted china!" she exclaimed. "Look at all those pink rosebuds!" She backed away. "I can't wash my face in that basin. I'd get the rosebuds dirty."

"That's what you're supposed to do," Lucy said. She turned slowly so she could look at everything in the room. There were lace curtains at the window and bright quilts on the beds. In one corner was a small writing desk and chair.

"Oh, how beautiful!" Lucy whispered.

Daisy's eyes brightened. "Do you think Mrs. Judson might want to adopt a girl?" She glanced at Lucy. "Maybe two girls?"

"Mrs. Judson could have chosen a child if she wanted to," Lucy said.

Daisy looked around the room again and sighed with delight. "Wouldn't this be a grand house to live in, Lucy?" she asked.

Lucy thought for just a moment. Then she said, "It is a grand house, but it doesn't have what I want in it. I want a mother and father and a little sister."

Daisy smiled. "There *is* a Mr. Judson," she said. "I heard somebody say he's a banker. So there's your mother and father. And I could be your little sister."

Lucy shook her head again, but she smiled. Mrs. Judson wasn't exactly what Lucy had hoped for in a mother, and Mr. Judson she hadn't seen at all. But Daisy would make a good little sister.

"Tomorrow morning I'm going to tell Mrs. Judson how happy her house would be with two daughters in it," Daisy said. "You'll have to smile, too. And be helpful."

"All right," Lucy said.

Daisy pulled off her shoes and dress and tossed them on the floor. Then she dove into bed. "Good night, Lucy," she said, and giggled. "To-morrow we may have a new mother."

Even though the early-evening sky was still light, Lucy was exhausted. She undressed. Then, sinking into the soft, beautiful bed, she pulled the quilt up to her chin.

Lucy wondered if Mrs. Judson would like chil-dren in her house. She and Daisy would be good, helpful daughters and do their best to make Mr. and Mrs. Judson happy parents. With a smile on her face, Lucy fell sound asleep.

The morning light awakened her. She jumped from bed, surprised to find that Daisy was already up and dressed.

Lucy washed her face and hands in the basin and put on her clothing.

"Should we fold the bed linens?" Daisy asked. "We want Mrs. Judson to think we're very helpful."

"We want her to think we're clean, too," Lucy said. "Wash your hands and face."

"You can't tell me what to do," Daisy complained.

"I can if I'm your big sister," Lucy said.

Daisy grumbled, but she quickly washed in the cool water. She even wiped up the splatters with her towel.

Lucy worked with Daisy to put the room in order. Then they hurried outside to the privy, remembering to wash their hands and dry them on the towel hanging outside the kitchen door.

The door opened, and a plump, middle-aged woman poked her head outside. "So this is where you got to," she said. "I was gonna start huntin' for the two of you if you didn't show up pretty soon." She smiled and said, "I'm Gussie, the Judsons' housekeeper."

"She has a housekeeper?" Daisy whispered to Lucy. She looked terribly disappointed. "We thought she might need a girl . . . uh . . . two girls to help out with the housework," Daisy told Gussie.

Gussie laughed. She poked a stray wisp of gray-blond hair back into the twist that sat like a fat biscuit on top of her head. "Last thing Mrs. Judson needs is two little girls. She has four of her own already and just married off the last one. What she wants now is to sleep late, like she's doin' this mornin'."

Gussie held the back door open wide. "You

come inside now. I'll fix your breakfast and get you to the depot in time for the train."

Lucy took Daisy's hand. "Don't be sad," she whispered. "We'll find our families. Maybe at the next stop."

"What if we don't?" Daisy whispered back.

Lucy remembered Miss Kelly's words. "You have to believe," Lucy said.

It was hard to believe and not be frightened. Lucy found that it was even harder not to give in to her fears when Gussie left her and Daisy at the train station. Lucy could see from the faces of the other children that they were just as terrified as she was.

Everyone looked sad. Everyone looked scared. No one had wanted them at the first stop. Would it be any different at the next stop?

A young couple rushed up to Miss Kelly. They had taken five-year-old Walter just to spend the night and had decided they wanted to keep him.

Lucy couldn't help feeling jealous. *There are*

only eleven of us now. She fought back a lump that stuck in her throat and made her want to cry.

In the distance she heard long blasts from the train's whistle. The train would be there soon, and they'd be on their way to Springbrook.

CHAPTER SEVEN

The train chugged through patches of woods and clearings. Lucy slumped against the uncomfortable wooden back of her seat. One hand gripped Baby. The other held tightly to Daisy, who huddled against her.

No one ran up and down the aisle. None of the boys teased. The car they rode in was quiet. Lucy was sure that everyone was thinking about the same thing: What would happen in Springbrook?

Lucy knew that Miss Kelly was trying to cheer them up. She told stories and sang and even made up riddles.

But every few minutes someone would ask,

"Will it be long until we get to Springbrook?" Or "Are we almost there?"

"In a little while," Miss Kelly would say patiently.

Then, finally, it was time to wash faces and hands, comb hair, and straighten jackets.

The conductor strode through the car. He called out, "Springbrook, next stop. Springbrook, five minutes."

Lucy found it hard to breathe. Her heart began to pound again as the train reached the depot. She saw a large cluster of people waiting on the platform.

Just as before, Lucy carried her parcel and Baby and climbed down the steps with the other children, following Miss Kelly.

A tall, thin woman shook hands with Miss Kelly. "I'm Isabelle Domain, chairman of Springbrook's placing-out committee," she said. "The train will be here for half an hour, so we'll do the choosing right here on the platform. Then we'll get the waifs no one wants back on board."

Lucy shuddered. Waifs? She wasn't a waif—especially not one that nobody would want. She was Lucy Amanda Griggs, and she'd find her parents here. She had to.

Lucy forced herself to stand up straight. She looked at the people who had come to see them. Each time she caught someone's eye, she smiled. She touched the marble in her pocket—her gift from Henry. Soon she'd have the gift of parents . . . and a sister.

Soon after the children had been introduced, they began to be chosen. A stout, middle-aged couple beamed at Daisy. The woman said, "A happy child brightens a lonely house. Will you come with us, Daisy? We'd be so thankful to have you as our little girl."

Daisy gave one quick, longing glance at Lucy. "Good-bye, Lucy," she said, then disappeared with her new parents into the crowd.

Lucy knew she should be happy for Daisy, but loneliness wiped away every other feeling. She hugged Baby and closed her eyes, choking back tears.

"Er . . . young lady . . . Lucy . . . ," a deep voice said.

Lucy opened her eyes. A man stood before her. He had sunbaked skin, with red blotches on his cheeks. His wide-brimmed hat shaded soft, kind eyes. He looked at her hopefully.

He said, "My name is Wilbur Snapes. My wife sent me to bring home an orphan girl to be a companion to our own little girl. Would you like to come with me?"

Miss Kelly stepped to Lucy's side. Before Lucy could answer, Miss Kelly asked, "Where is your wife, Mr. Snapes? I'd like to meet her."

"Mabel couldn't come," Mr. Snapes said. "She had to stay home to take care of the child."

"I'm not sure that—" Miss Kelly began, but Lucy quickly spoke up.

"Miss Kelly, they have a little girl!" Lucy said.

"I'd have a little sister! This is what I wanted right from the beginning!" She looked up at Mr. Snapes. "What's your little girl's name?"

"Emma," he answered.

"Emma!" Lucy gave a happy sigh. "That's a lovely name!"

Mrs. Domain joined them. She nodded to Mr. Snapes. "Morning, Wilbur," she said. She turned to Miss Kelly. "The Snapeses are good-hearted people. I recommend them."

"We usually meet *both* parents," Miss Kelly said. But Mrs. Domain shook her head.

"Poor Mabel doesn't get out much, what with Emma to care for. But she's a fine, upstanding woman. Did I mention that Wilbur's a deacon in our church?"

Miss Kelly took Lucy aside. "Are you sure you want to live with the Snapeses?" she asked. "You have a choice."

Lucy looked over her shoulder at Mr. Snapes and into his kind eyes. A sister! Her wish was finally coming true.

"I choose *yes,*" she said to Miss Kelly. "I'm going to have a sister!"

Miss Kelly smiled at Lucy. "All right. We'll give Mr. Snapes the papers to sign."

Signing only took a few minutes. Mr. Snapes put down the pen and ink and nodded to Lucy. "This way," he said.

But Lucy took time to wrap herself in Miss Kelly's hug.

"Write to me," Miss Kelly said. "I want to know that you're happy. Will you let me know?"

"Yes," Lucy promised. "I will."

She pulled away and followed Mr. Snapes to a large farm wagon. He boosted her to the board seat, where she found herself perched high behind two large horses.

"Tell me about Emma," Lucy said to Mr. Snapes excitedly.

There was a long pause before he answered. "Emma's a good little girl, a loving girl. You'll see for yourself when you meet her."

Lucy soon realized that Mr. Snapes was not a

talker. That was all right with her. At the moment she was so filled with excitement she didn't feel like talking, either. *Someone to love me. My wish has come true. I'll have someone to love me,* she thought.

As they left Springbrook and entered a quiet country road, Mr. Snapes asked, "Would you like to hold the horses' reins?"

"Oh, yes!" Lucy said.

Mr. Snapes showed her how to hold the reins and told her what commands to give the horses. Then he sat quietly by her side.

He's a kind man, Lucy thought, *and that's what counts.*

As the horses plodded on, Lucy gazed at the countryside. She loved the rolling hills and the tidy farmland.

When Mr. Snapes took the reins and guided his horses up a road to a small farmhouse, Lucy was delighted. The house was part of her wish, and her wish was coming true.

The wagon stopped, and Lucy quickly jumped

down from the seat. She was eager to meet Mrs. Snapes. Would she be as nice as Mr. Snapes?

But the middle-aged woman who stepped onto the front porch didn't have a welcoming smile on her face. Her lips were tight and angry, and her forehead was creased into a frown. She stared at Lucy and snapped, "She's too small, Wilbur. Take her back."

Mr. Snapes shook his head firmly. "No, Mabel. I won't. You sent back the last one because she was running around the house making noise and upsetting Emma. 'Don't bring me any girls who act like boys,' you told me. Well Lucy won't. She's a quiet little thing. She'll do. You'll see."

Lucy was so shocked she leaned against the wagon for support. Sent back? Their last orphan train rider was sent back? This wasn't the way her wish was supposed to turn out. Where was the smiling mother? Where was her dear little sister? Where was the love?

CHAPTER EIGHT

"Take Lucy inside, Mabel," Mr. Snapes said quickly. "Lucy and Emma should get to know each other."

Numbly Lucy walked up the porch steps and into the house. There, on a sofa, sat a girl who was probably twelve or thirteen. There was something different about her eyes, as if they didn't see things the way other people did. Her lower lip sagged, too. But she perked up when she saw Lucy.

With a start, Lucy realized that Emma seemed to be very much like Mrs. Olney's Henry. Especially her eyes. What was it that Mum had said?

That Henry was simple. Lucy was sure that Emma was simple, too. She was older than Lucy and much larger. Emma was not the cuddly little sister of her daydreams.

"This here is Lucy," Mrs. Snapes said to Emma. "She's come to live with us and help take care of you."

Lucy remembered Henry and how much he needed and wanted kindness. She smiled and said, "Hello, Emma."

Emma smiled, too, and climbed from the sofa. Her walk was clumsy and slow. As she came close to Lucy, her arms reached out and she took Lucy's hand. "Play outside," Emma said.

When Mrs. Snapes didn't say anything, Lucy looked up at her. "Emma said she wants to go outside to play."

Mrs. Snapes sighed. "Emma just makes noises. She doesn't know how to talk. So don't start imagining that you know what she says. We just let her babble on and keep doing what's best for her."

Maybe that's what you *do,* Lucy thought. *But I know what I heard. Emma asked to go outside to play.* Mum had been able to understand Henry, and Lucy had learned, too.

Lucy tried to remember the things Mrs. Olney had said about Henry. "Has Emma been like this since she was born?"

Mrs. Snapes's mouth grew even tighter. "Yes," she muttered. "It was a difficult birth, but that's neither here nor there. Can't nothing at all be done about it. Come with me, and I'll show you your room. You'll share it with Emma."

It was a large room, but the tan-and-brown wallpaper made it look dark and dreary. Lucy thought the wallpaper was ugly. But Mrs. Snapes said, "I see you're admiring the paper. It cost dearly, but no one's going to say we didn't do our best for Emma."

Lucy put her parcel on the bed and opened it. She shook out the dress that had been packed inside and hung it inside the wardrobe. Then she put her change of underwear into the cupboard drawer Mrs. Snapes had opened.

"Only one pair of shoes?" Mrs. Snapes asked. "Well, can't say I didn't expect it." She pointed at the shoes Lucy was wearing and said, "You can save those for Sundays. Until it turns cold, you can do what most of the children around here do—go barefoot."

"Yes, ma'am," Lucy answered.

Emma picked up Baby. She mumbled something, but Lucy easily picked out one word: "Doll."

"Yes," Lucy said. "She's my doll. Her name is Baby."

"Baby," Emma said.

"That's right. Baby," Lucy answered.

"I don't know that it's good for Emma to have you pretend to understand her," Mrs. Snapes said.

"But I did understand her," Lucy said. "She said 'doll' and 'Baby.'"

"Nonsense," Mrs. Snapes said. Lucy could see

the pain in her eyes. "No one's ever been able to understand Emma. She makes sounds, but she'll never be able to speak words. It's like I told you. Her brain was damaged when she was born."

"Back in New York City there was a boy named Henry," Lucy said. "Mum could talk to Henry. He was . . . well . . . like Emma. Mum taught me to really listen to what Henry said. I could understand him, and I can understand Emma too."

Lucy could see that Mrs. Snapes didn't believe her. "Let's get things straight, right from the start," Mrs. Snapes said. "You'll have regular chores, just as if you was one of the family. You'll help with the tidying up and weekly cleaning. You'll make Emma's bed and yours each morning and change the sheets on Fridays. You'll lend a hand with the washing, too. And you'll set the table and do the dishes after every meal. In September you'll go to school. I don't much like the schooling part, but rules are rules."

Just when Lucy thought that Mrs. Snapes was

through, she added, "And you'll watch over Emma. Keep her busy so she won't be into tantrums or breaking things. Keep her happy."

Partly closed curtains darkened the bedroom. But through the sun-streaked glass Lucy could see a garden and green grass.

"May I take Emma outside to play?" Lucy asked.

Mrs. Snapes thought a moment, then nodded. "If you watch her closely," she said. "Don't go near the well, even when it's covered. And stay away from the near pasture where Mr. Snapes brings the bull to graze."

Lucy held out a hand to Emma, who took it eagerly. They followed Mrs. Snapes down the stairs and through the large kitchen to the backyard. Lucy went right to the vegetable garden, hungry to taste the good things growing there.

Before Lucy could stop her, Emma pulled up two carrots. "Oh, no," Lucy said. "How do we put them back?"

Emma gave one carrot to Lucy. Then she slapped the other carrot against her thigh, knocking off the dirt. With a loud crunch, she bit into the end of the carrot and began to chew.

Lucy did the same. The fresh, juicy, crisp carrot tasted better than any carrot she'd ever eaten in her whole life.

Lucy led Emma to a back-porch swing. Holding Baby, Lucy rocked and patted her as she sang, "Rock, rock, my baby-o. Rock, rock, my baby."

When the song was finished, Emma grinned and clapped her hands. "Baby-o," she said.

"All right. I'll sing it again," Lucy said. "My mum sang that song to me when I was sleepy or sad."

Emma reached out toward Lucy, her fingers wiggling.

Lucy caught the hand and stroked the fingers until they were still. Then she laid them against her cheek. "You don't know what sad is, do you, Emma?" she asked, as if she were talking to herself. "Sad is not having a mother and father anymore. Sad is wishing for new parents—happy people to love, with a baby sister to cuddle."

Lucy's voice cracked. A tear rolled down her cheek and onto Emma's finger. "Sad is making a wish and finding that it will never come true," Lucy said.

Emma pulled her hand away and studied the wet spot on her finger. Then she tugged on Lucy's arm, saying, "Baby-o."

Lucy sang the song over and over again for Emma, until the back door swung open. Mrs. Snapes called out, "Lucy? Time to bring Emma inside. There's potatoes to scrub and the table to set."

"Come on, Emma," Lucy said. She jumped up and pulled Emma to her feet.

Lucy was glad to help with the supper and cleaning up. It was only fair to do her share in exchange for living in a cozy house with good food to eat. She was ready to try out her bed, too. It had been a long day, and she was tired.

But after supper, Mrs. Snapes handed Lucy a metal hoop and a needle and thread. "Idle hours are wasted hours," she said. "Before bedtime you can embroider a sampler."

"I don't know how to embroider," Lucy said.

Mrs. Snapes's eyebrows rose in surprise. "You've never made a sampler?"

Embarrassed, Lucy shook her head.

Mrs. Snapes sighed. "I suppose I should have expected it. Well, it's about time you learned."

Mr. Snapes put down his book and said, "Mabel, the child's worn out. Why don't you let Lucy and Emma go to bed? You can teach Lucy needlework tomorrow."

Mrs. Snapes studied Lucy intently. "You do look tired," she said. "Can you help Emma to the privy? Afterward, you can wash her hands and face and help her into her nightgown."

"I can do that," Lucy said. She was eager to escape.

Emma seemed happy to please Lucy. She giggled when Lucy made a game of washing her face.

Lucy drew soap circles on Emma's cheeks, nose, and chin.

I wonder if Mr. or Mrs. Snapes has ever tried playing with Emma, Lucy wondered.

Lucy helped Emma into bed, smoothing back her hair and tucking the quilt under her chin. "Good night, Emma," she said.

Emma smiled as Lucy blew out the oil lamp that stood on the table.

In the dark Lucy changed into her nightgown and climbed into bed, holding Baby. She was so tired that she thought she would fall asleep as soon as she closed her eyes.

Instead, she lay awake. She looked at the patterns of moonlight that shone through the window and listened to Emma breathe. This was the same moonlight that had streamed through the small window in the room she had shared with her mother in New York City. Sometimes Mum had snuggled with her, pointing out shapes and designs in the spots of moonlight that had brightened the table and floor.

"Oh, Mum, I miss you. I miss you so much," Lucy whispered. She hugged Baby and wished with all her heart that Mum hadn't died, and that they were still together. The idea of living forever with unhappy Mrs. Snapes made her begin to cry. She couldn't stop the tears, and she hid her head under the quilt so she wouldn't awaken Emma.

Suddenly she felt a hand on her shoulder. "Baby-o," Emma said softly, and began to pat Lucy. "Baby-o, Baby-o."

CHAPTER NINE

During the next few days Lucy worked hard on her household chores. She thought she must be pleasing Mrs. Snapes, because Mrs. Snapes did not complain. Every day Lucy helped Emma dress and undress. She sat beside Emma during meals and helped her eat.

"Hold the spoon like this, Emma," Lucy said. "Then you won't spill."

Mrs. Snapes frowned. "That's not the proper way to hold a spoon," she said.

"Yes, ma'am, I know it's not proper," Lucy said politely. She was glad Mum had taught her good manners. "But it's easier for Emma."

Mr. Snapes looked up from the soup he was spooning into his mouth. He watched Emma, who was happily eating her soup with her fist gripping her spoon. "It makes good sense to me," he said.

Mrs. Snapes just shrugged and sighed.

Lucy spent hours of play time with Emma. She took Emma walking. She sat with her on the grass, weaving dandelion crowns. She told Emma stories and sang to her. Lucy let Emma hold her marble, and she told her about Henry. And sometimes—when Emma was paying attention—Lucy tried to teach her new words. Emma couldn't always learn them. But even without the words, Lucy could understand what Emma wanted and needed.

On Sunday Lucy went to church with the Snapeses.

"You'll meet some of the other children," Mrs. Snapes told her as their wagon came near the church grounds. "Come September, you'll be going to school with them."

Lucy was excited. She couldn't wait to make friends with the girls her age.

Mrs. Snapes had filled a big basket with fried chicken, slices of ham, fluffy biscuits, carrots, and jars of pickles. "After services there'll be dinner on the ground," she said.

"What's dinner on the ground?" Lucy asked.

"We all spread out cloths and sit down on the ground to eat," Mrs. Snapes answered. "There'll be fiddlers and we'll sing hymns. It's a time for neighbors to get together. We do this once a month, in good weather."

As Lucy followed the Snapeses into church, Emma clung tightly to her hand. Lucy could hear whispers and even a few giggles. Some of the children stared at her.

It's because I'm new here, Lucy told herself.

After the services, some of the children clustered around Lucy and Emma.

"You're the new orphan," a girl with long blond hair said.

Lucy tried to smile. "I'm Lucy. Lucy Griggs."

A little boy tugged at the blond girl's skirt. "What's an orphan?" he asked.

"An orphan is somebody who has no mother or father," the girl answered.

The boy looked puzzled. "How could you not have a mother or father?"

A bigger boy grinned at Lucy. "Orphans aren't like the rest of us. Orphans are found under rocks."

One of the other girls giggled. "So was Emma," she said. "They make a fine pair."

Everyone laughed. Lucy could tell that Emma didn't understand what they said or why they were laughing, but Emma laughed with them anyway. And this made the other children laugh even harder.

Lucy's face burned with anger and embarrassment. It was bad enough that her wish hadn't come true. Now it seemed as though she wouldn't have a single friend. She took Emma's hand and began to walk away. "Come on, Emma," she said.

They found Mrs. Snapes dishing up heaping plates of food, all the while keeping an eye on what her neighbors had brought. "You weren't very pleasant with the other children," she said to Lucy. "Look at them all laughing and playing. Why didn't you join in?"

Before Lucy could explain, Mr. Snapes said, "Lucy's shy, Mabel. Give her time. She'll make friends."

Even though she wasn't hungry, Lucy bit into a chicken leg. It tasted like straw. There was no way she could tell the Snapeses what the children had said. The part about Emma would only hurt the Snapeses. It was her problem, and she'd have to handle it herself.

On the following Sunday, Mrs. Snapes announced, "After church we'll be having dinner at the home of some relations." To Lucy's surprise, after the services she found out that the blond girls and the tall boy who had taunted her and Emma were Emma's cousins.

Mrs. Snapes made the introductions. "This

here is Lucy," she said. "And these are my sister Grace Porter's children—Janetta, Abigail, and Tom."

"Pleased to meet you," they all said politely. Abigail even bobbed up and down in a curtsy.

Don't they remember last Sunday? Lucy wondered.

"Seems like the cat's got Lucy's tongue," Mrs. Snapes prompted.

Lucy quickly said, "How do you do?"

Mrs. Porter was a small good-natured woman. She smiled and said, "We're glad to have you here, Lucy." She turned to the others. "Children, go outside and play. You won't have any fun inside, under the grown-ups' feet."

Lucy, with Emma in hand, followed the Porter children to a shady area under an oak tree.

Emma plopped down on the grass. Tom said, "Emma, do you want little, sizzly fried bugs for dinner?"

Emma smiled and nodded, and Tom's sisters giggled.

"Or how about a lizard? A roasted and stuffed lizard? Isn't that what you usually eat?"

Janetta and Abigail laughed. Emma laughed with them.

"Stop it," Lucy said.

Tom looked at Lucy with surprise. "Stop what?"

"Stop making fun of Emma," Lucy said.

"Why?" Abigail asked. "She doesn't know we're making fun of her."

"But *you* do, and that's just plain mean."

"It's only teasing. We always do it," Abigail insisted. She looked at her brother and giggled. "Tom can be so funny!"

"If it's so funny, do you tease Emma in front of your parents and hers so they can laugh, too?" Lucy asked.

For a moment there was silence. Then Janetta asked Lucy, "Are you going to be an old spoilsport? Are you going to tattle?"

"I don't tattle," Lucy said. "But one of my jobs

is to take care of Emma. I want you to stop making fun of her."

Tom, Janetta, and Abigail looked at one another. Then Abigail's pout turned into a smile. "Oh, let's stop talking about Emma," Abigail said. "We brought you here to show you our secret treasure hole, Lucy."

Abigail reached into a hole in the trunk of the tree and pulled out a box. Opening it, she held up a sleek black feather.

"A crow's feather?" Lucy asked.

Janetta shook her head and whispered, "A magic feather. *Bad* magic. All we need is to find the spell."

"Where's the spell?"

Janetta sighed. "We don't know."

"We'll know it when we see it," Tom said.

"But why do you want to do *bad* magic?" Lucy asked.

"Just because," said Abigail. "Don't ask so many questions."

"All right," Lucy said. She was interested in what else lay in the box.

There was a three-inch rattle, taken from a dead rattlesnake; a small gold ring; a dead and dried frog; and five agate marbles—lucky marbles, Tom said.

"Now we've shown you our treasures," Abigail said. "That means we're friends."

"Friends? Really?" Lucy asked.

"Wait," Tom said. "We haven't shown Lucy our secret handshake."

He held out his right hand, thumb up, and he and Abigail slapped hands and shook. Then they showed Lucy how to do the same.

"That does it," Tom said. "Now we're friends, and we stick together, no matter what."

Lucy smiled. She was glad to have friends. And best of all, she got to share their secret.

Emma looked up and babbled something. Lucy tried to catch a word she could understand, but she couldn't.

"Emma, when you grow up, why don't you

join a group of traveling actors?" Tom said. He bowed as if he were on a stage. Then he began to babble, making fun of Emma.

Abigail and Janetta both burst out laughing.

Then Emma joined in, laughing loudly.

Abigail threw a glance at Lucy.

Lucy didn't know what to do. Emma was laughing. And after all, these were her new friends. All the laughing made Lucy want to laugh, too. Before she knew it, she was giggling. Abigail squeezed her hand in delight.

Janetta put an arm around Lucy's shoulder. "Friends," Janetta whispered in Lucy's ear.

Tom, Janetta, and Abigail were right, Lucy told herself. Emma was laughing. The teasing didn't hurt her.

But late that evening, as the Snapeses rode home, Lucy thought about what she had done. In the back of the wagon, Emma snuggled against Lucy. Lucy thought she heard Emma say, "Love you."

Lucy hugged Emma. She felt sick as she remembered laughing at her. Emma had trusted her, and she had betrayed her—all for the sake of having friends.

But Emma didn't know she was being made fun of, so she wasn't hurt, Lucy told herself. *I didn't really do anything wrong . . . did I?*

CHAPTER TEN

Two days later Abigail and Janetta arrived with their mother for a visit at the Snapeses' farm. Lucy wasn't happy to see them. No matter what the girls had told her, Lucy knew they weren't her real friends.

Mrs. Porter's arms were filled with printed fabric. She was going to sew kitchen curtains. "You're kind to help me hem these, Mabel," Mrs. Porter said.

"The girls can help, too," Mrs. Snapes said. "With five of us at work, we'll be done in no time."

Mrs. Porter smiled at her daughters. "Let's just you and me hem them, Mabel," she said. "The girls do so hate to sew. We'll send them all outside to play."

Mrs. Porter shooed Lucy, Emma, Janetta, and Abigail out the back door. Lucy could tell that Mrs. Snapes didn't like the idea.

Lucy didn't like the idea, either. She was still ashamed of laughing while Tom made fun of Emma. Thankfully, Tom hadn't come, so maybe Abigail and Janetta would leave Emma alone.

They were no sooner away from the house than Abigail began to make fun of Emma. "Big old Emma's still got a dolly."

She and Janetta laughed, but Emma held up Baby and spoke back to them. Lucy could pick out the words *Baby* and *doll.*

"She's telling you that the doll is named Baby," Lucy said.

Janetta and Abigail exploded in laughter. "Emma can't talk!" Janetta said.

"And don't tell us that you can understand her!" Abigail screeched.

Lucy took a deep breath. "Don't tease her," she said.

"Why not?" Abigail answered. "Emma doesn't know what we're talking about. It's so funny when she laughs with us."

"It isn't right," Lucy insisted.

"There you go being a spoilsport again," Janetta said. "Come on. Let's play a game."

She snatched Baby out of Emma's arms and ran toward the bull's pasture. By the time Lucy realized what was happening, Janetta had tossed Baby into the pasture.

"No! No!" Lucy cried. As she watched, horrified, Janetta climbed through the rail fence, dashed to the doll, picked it up, and ran back.

The bull, in the distance, raised his head and snorted.

Both Emma and Lucy reached for the doll, but

Abigail grabbed it. "My turn," she said. She tossed the doll into the pasture and climbed through the fence to go after it, imitating her sister.

"Come back! Hurry!" Lucy cried as the bull trotted a little closer.

Laughing, Abigail ran to the fence and squeezed through the rails.

With a cry Emma again reached for the doll, but Abigail held it high. "Your turn," she said to Lucy.

"No," Lucy said, shuddering. "Don't do that!" She watched the bull. He seemed to stare right at her. "The bull's closer now. I'm not going in there."

"Yes, you are," Abigail cried. She threw Baby into the pasture. "I said, it's your turn."

"And I told you no," Lucy said. "The bull's too close. Besides, you threw it farther in than you did for yourself."

"Did not."

"Did too."

Lucy was so angry at Abigail, she forgot about watching Emma. It wasn't until Janetta gasped and pointed that Lucy turned and saw Emma in the pasture, stumbling through the grass toward the doll.

The bull raised his head. He snorted loudly and pawed the ground, kicking up clods of dirt.

Abigail and Janetta ran screaming toward the house. But Lucy knew that help couldn't possibly come in time. She ducked through the fence rails and raced toward Emma. Emma had picked up Baby and was standing quietly, cuddling the doll.

From the corner of her eye Lucy saw the bull come a few steps closer. She grabbed Emma's hand and tugged her toward the fence. Emma stumbled, but Lucy half-pulled, half-carried her, moving as quickly as possible.

Lucy could see Mr. Snapes running toward them. He shouted at the bull, waving his arms. Behind him raced the others, screaming in terror.

The thumping steps of the bull grew louder as he thundered closer.

In a last burst of speed, Lucy reached the fence and pushed Emma through. She glanced over her shoulder and saw that the bull was almost on top of her. She threw herself to one side as the bull's horns sideswiped the top rail of the fence. Then she dove through the gap between the two bottom rails. She didn't have time to be careful. She hit her head hard on the upper rail.

"Emma? Is Emma all right?" Lucy tried to ask, but her head hurt too much. She sailed into blackness.

She awoke to feel gentle hands stroking her forehead. She heard a soft voice say, "I love you, Lucy. I love you."

"Mum?" Lucy asked. "Is it you?" She tried to wake up.

The blackness went away. Lucy opened her eyes. She was lying on the ground outside the pasture, her head in Emma's lap. "Love you," Emma was saying.

"She's been babbling to you ever since you

fainted," Mrs. Snapes said to Lucy. "It seems you're all right now."

"The bull?" Lucy asked.

"The bull didn't touch you. You just bumped your head."

Lucy sat up carefully. Her head still hurt, but that didn't matter. She knew what Emma had said. Her wish really had come true. She wrapped her arms around Emma and murmured in her ear, "I love you, too."

Abigail was wiping her tears on her sleeve. "It was all Janetta's fault," she cried. "She threw the doll into the pasture."

"Did not!" Janetta screeched. "Abigail did it!"

"Did not!"

"Did too!"

"You're all to blame," said their mother angrily. "Get in the buggy, daughters. We're going home."

"Please don't tell Father," Abigail begged.

Mrs. Porter thought a moment, then shrugged.

"Well . . . ," she said. Her voice trailed off as she walked toward her buggy. "Since no harm's been done . . ."

Lucy was heartsick. "I'm sorry," she said to Mr. and Mrs. Snapes. "You told me to keep Emma away from the pasture, and I didn't." Tears came to her eyes. She added, "If you want to send me back, I . . . I . . ."

"Send you back? When I've just got used to you? What nonsense," Mrs. Snapes said. "Besides, you have a knack with Emma. No one else has ever made her so happy."

"You were very brave to try to save our Emma," Mr. Snapes said, putting his hand on Lucy's shoulder. "We're grateful to you."

Mrs. Snapes's face reddened, and her voice grew husky. "We're . . . we're glad you're here, Lucy."

"Thank you," Lucy said, and she smiled.

Mrs. Snapes hesitated, as if she wanted to reach out and pat Lucy's arm. But instead she straightened up. "Well, there's no point in standing around out here when there's chores to be done. I must collect the eggs. You ought to lie down before you set the table for supper."

Lucy gingerly touched the lump on her forehead. It would probably turn red and purple and look a sight, but it didn't hurt as much as it had.

She got up, grabbed Emma's hand, and followed the Snapeses to the house. As she walked, she smiled to herself. She might not have found the family of her dreams. And when school began there would still be unkind remarks from the boys and girls in her class. There would be many times when she'd have to stand up for herself and for Emma. But her wish had come true.

Maybe even Mrs. Snapes would give her more than a thank-you. One day Lucy might get a smile and a hug—just like Emma had already given her.

Lucy grinned with excitement. She had someone to love her—someone whom she'd always love in return. She and Emma would always have each other.

Epilogue
Letter from Lucy Griggs
to Frances Mary Kelly

Dear Miss Kelly,

On our journey to Missouri I had a secret wish. When I was placed out with the Snapeses I thought it had come true, and then I was afraid it hadn't. I found out that I was looking in the wrong place! I now know that even though only a part of my wish came true, that was enough. Because the part that came true was the important part.

I do have a sister. I love my sister, Emma, and Emma loves me. That makes us both happy. The word people use for Emma is "simple." Mrs. Snapes said there's nothing that can be done about it. I'm not so sure she's right. I'm teaching Emma more words to say. I'm going to teach her to say them slowly and plainly so that everyone can understand her, not just me. That may not seem like much, but it will be important to Emma. And to me. I also know my mum would be happy that I am doing this.

I love living in Missouri after all. Have you heard from Daisy? Please write to me. I hope that you are well and that your wishes also come true. Thank you for your kindness, Miss Kelly.

Yours very truly,

Lucy Amanda Griggs

Glossary

camisole *kam'-i-sol* A short, sleeveless garment worn over a girl's or woman's underwear, under her dress or blouse.

cholera *kol'-er-a* An infectious, often fatal disease.

committee *ka-mit'-e* A group of people elected or appointed to perform a service.

embroider *em-broi'-der* To sew a design on a piece of fabric with needlework.

evict *e-vikt'* To legally remove someone from the property on which he or she is living.

fort *fort* A military site, strengthened to prevent attack and occupied by soldiers.

frock coat *frok cot* A man's close-fitting coat, long enough to reach the knees.

hem *hem* To fold back and sew down the edge of a piece of cloth.

pallet *pal'-it* A small, makeshift bed of blankets or straw.

parasol *par'-e-sol* A woman's sun umbrella.

placed out *plased out* The term used by the Children's Aid Society to mean that a home had been found for a child on an orphan train.

privy *priv'-e* An outside toilet.

refuse *ref'-yoos* Something that is discarded as useless. Trash or garbage.

sampler *sam'-pler* An embroidered cloth showing a beginner's talent with the needle.

tenement *ten'-a-ment* An apartment house in the poorest, most crowded part of a city.

top hat *top hat* A man's tall hat with a curved brim. Often made of silk.

waif *waf* A child who has no home or friends.

well *wel* A hole drilled or dug into the earth to get water.

The Story of
the Orphan Trains

In 1850 there were five hundred thousand people living in New York City. Ten thousand of these people were homeless children.

Many of these children were immigrants—they had come to the United States with their families from other countries. Many lived in one-room apartments. These rooms had stoves for heating and cooking, but the only water was in troughs in the hallways. These apartments were called tenements, and they were often crowded together in neighborhoods.

Immigrant parents worked long hours for very low wages. Sometimes they had barely enough money to buy food. Everyone in the family over the age of ten was expected to work. Few of these children could attend school, and many could not read or write.

Girls took in bundles of cloth from clothing

New York City's Lower East Side during the late nineteenth century.
Courtesy the Children's Aid Society

manufacturers. They carefully sewed men's shirts, women's blouses, and babies' gowns. Or they made paper flowers and tried to sell them on the busy streets.

Boys shined shoes or sold newspapers.

There were no wonder medicines in the 1800s. Many immigrants who lived in poor conditions died from contagious diseases. Children often became orphans with no one to care for them.

Some orphaned children were taken in by aunts and uncles. But many of the immigrant children had no relatives to come to their aid. They had left their grandparents, aunts, and uncles in other countries. They were alone. No one in the government had developed any plans for caring for them.

These orphans were evicted from their homes so that the rooms could be rented to other families. Orphans with no homes and no beds slept in alleys.

This was a time in which children were expected to work hard, along with adults. They

A New York City "street arab."
Courtesy the Children's Aid Society

were expected to take care of themselves. But there were not enough jobs for all the orphans in New York City. Many street arabs, as they were called, turned to lives of crime.

Charles Loring Brace, a young minister and social worker, became aware of this situation. He worried about these children, who so badly needed care. With the help of some friends he founded the Children's Aid Society. The Children's Aid Society provided a place to live for some of the homeless children. It also set up industrial schools to train the children of the very poor in job skills.

Charles Loring Brace soon realized, however, that these steps were not enough. He came up with the idea of giving homeless, orphaned children a second—and much better—chance at life by taking them out of the city and placing them in homes in rural areas of the country.

Brace hired a scout to visit some of the farm communities west of New York State. He asked the scout to find out if people would be interested

Charles Loring Brace, founder of the Children's Aid Society
and the orphan train program.
Courtesy the Children's Aid Society

A boy proudly holds up his Children's Aid Society membership card.
Courtesy the Children's Aid Society

in taking orphan children into their homes. The scout was surprised by how many people wanted the children.

One woman wrote, "Last year was a very hard year, and we lost many of our children. Yes, we want your children. Please send your children."

Brace went to orphans who were living on the

streets and told them what he wanted to do. Children flocked to the Children's Aid Society office. "Take me," they begged. "Please take me."

"Where do you live?" the children were asked.

The answer was always the same: "Don't live nowhere."

The first orphan train was sent west in 1856, and the last one in 1929. During these years more than a hundred and fifty thousand children were taken out of New York City by the Children's Aid Society. Another hundred thousand children were sent by train to new homes in the West by the New York Foundling Home. By 1929, states had established welfare laws and had begun taking care of people in need, so the orphan trains were discontinued.

Before a group of children was sent west by train, notices that the children were coming would be placed in the newspapers of towns along the route: "WANTED: HOMES FOR CHILDREN," one notice said. It then listed the Society's rules. Children were to be treated as members of the

Boys on board an orphan train.
Courtesy the Children's Aid Society

family. They were to be taken to church on Sundays and sent to school until they were fourteen.

Handbills were posted in the towns where the orphan train stopped, where people could easily see them. One said: "CHILDREN WITHOUT HOMES. A number of the Children brought from

New York are still without homes. Friends from the country, please call and see them."

A committee of local citizens would be chosen at each of the towns. The members of the committee were given the responsibility of making sure that the people who took the orphan train children in were good people.

Most committee members tried to do a good job. But sometimes a child was placed in a home that turned out to be unhappy. Some farmers wanted free labor and were unkind to the boys they chose. But there were many good people who wanted to provide loving homes for the orphans. Many people were so happy with their children that they took a step beyond being foster parents and legally adopted them.

Not all the children who were taken west on the orphan trains were orphans. Some had one or both parents still living. But sometimes fathers and mothers brought their children to the Children's Aid Society.

Families that wanted to adopt an orphan train rider
had to follow rules such as these.
Courtesy the Children's Aid Society

"I can't take care of my children," they would say. "I want them to have a much better life than I can give them. Please take them west to a new home."

What did the orphan train children think about their new lives? What made the biggest impression on them? They were used to living in small spaces, surrounded by many people in a

A group of children ready to board the orphan trains,
and their placing-out agents.
Courtesy the Children's Aid Society

noisy, crowded city. Were they overwhelmed by
the sight of miles of open countryside?

Many of them had never tasted an apple. How
did they react when they saw red apples growing
on trees?

When they sat down to a meal with their new families, did they stuff themselves? And did they feel a little guilty, remembering the small portions of food their parents had to eat?

Were they afraid to approach the large farm animals? What was it like for them to milk a cow for the first time?

During the first few years of the orphan trains, the records kept by the Children's Aid Society were not complete. In 1917 an agent made a survey. He wanted to find out what had happened to many of the orphan train children who had grown up.

He found that among them were a governor of North Dakota, a governor of the Territory of Alaska, two members of the United States Congress, nine members of state legislatures, two district attorneys, two mayors, a justice of the Supreme Court, four judges, many college professors, teachers, journalists, bankers, doctors, attorneys, four army officers, and seven thousand soldiers and sailors.

WHAT IS NEEDED

Money is needed to carry forward this great child-saving enterprise. With more confidence do we ask it, since it has been so clearly shown that this work of philanthropy is not a dead weight upon the community. Though its chief aim is to rescue the helpless child victims of our social errors, it also makes a distinct economic return in the reduction of the number of those who are hopeless charges upon the common purse. More money at our command means more power to extend this great opportunity of help to the many homeless children in the boys' and girls' lodging houses in New York, and in the asylums and institutions throughout the State. We therefore ask the public for a more liberal support of this noble charity, confident that every dollar invested will bring a double return in the best kind of help to the children, so pitifully in need of it.

TABLE SHOWING THE NUMBER OF CHILDREN AND POOR FAMILIES SENT TO EACH STATE

New York	33,053	North Dakota	975
New Jersey	4,977	South Dakota	43
Pennsylvania	2,679	Kentucky	212
Maryland	563	Georgia	317
Delaware	833	Tennessee	233
District of Columbia	172	Mississippi	210
Canada	566	Florida	600
Maine	43	Alabama	50
New Hampshire	136	North Carolina	144
Vermont	262	South Carolina	191
Rhode Island	340	Louisiana	70
Massachusetts	375	Indian Territory	59
Connecticut	1,588	Oklahoma	95
Ohio	7,272	Arkansas	136
Indiana	3,955	Montana	83
Illinois	9,172	Wyoming	19
Iowa	6,675	Colorado	1,563
Missouri	6,088	Utah	31
Nebraska	3,442	Idaho	52
Minnesota	3,258	Washington	231
Kansas	4,150	Nevada	59
Michigan	5,326	Oregon	90
Wisconsin	2,750	California	168
Virginia	1,634	New Mexico	1
West Virginia	149	Texas	1,527

This chart, from the Children's Aid Society's 1910 bulletin, shows the number of children who rode the orphan trains and the states to which they were sent.
Courtesy the Children's Aid Society

Although there were some problems in this system of matching homeless children with foster parents, the orphan train program did what it set out to do. It gave the homeless children of New York City the chance to live much better lives.

Three sisters who were taken in by the Children's Aid Society after their mother had died. At the time the photograph was taken, the two youngest girls had been adopted.
Courtesy the Children's Aid Society

New York City in the 1860s

New York City in the 1860s was a fast-paced, crowded, and sometimes dangerous city. Almost half the population of the city had been born in another country. Most of these immigrants came from Ireland or Germany.

The streets of New York City were full of life. Food and other items were sold in markets, and children played marbles and other outdoor games. Horse-drawn carriages clattered noisily down the bumpy streets, which were paved with cobblestones.

Many of the people who settled in New York City in the 1860s moved to the southern part of Manhattan. There they could be close to the factories and docks where they worked. They lived in tenements—cheaply built, overcrowded housing. People in tenements used outdoor communal toilets that often overflowed and enabled diseases like cholera to spread quickly.

A New York City street scene.
Courtesy the Children's Aid Society

In fact, in 1866, the year in which *Lucy's Wish* is set, one of the most serious epidemics of cholera in history hit New York City. There were eleven hundred deaths in 1866 alone; there were sixteen hundred deaths between 1860 and 1870. And it was usually poor immigrants, like Lucy's mother, who died from cholera, or from tuberculosis or scarlet fever.

New York City in the 1860s was a violent place. There was tension between longtime residents and new immigrants, between the rich and the poor, and between people of different ethnic backgrounds. Immigrants were blamed for the cholera epidemic and for taking jobs from others by agreeing to work for lower wages. These tensions led to riots. There were also violent protests against the draft for the Civil War. In 1863, one of these protests turned into a terrible riot in which hundreds of New Yorkers were killed or wounded.

There were public schools in New York City in the 1860s, but many poor and immigrant children could not attend them. There simply wasn't room in the schools for the huge number of immigrant children, and many were turned away. Some schools operated two half-day sessions so that more children could attend. Younger chil-

Two New York City children in their tenement home.
Between them is a Christmas tree they have made
using a broom and a bucket.
Courtesy the Children's Aid Society

These boys stand on a New York City street, ready to travel west
and start new lives. Their placing-out agent stands behind them.
Courtesy the Children's Aid Society

dren were taught arithmetic, singing, drawing,
calisthenics, and English. Older students also
studied science, history, and civics. There was no
public high-school system in New York City at
that time, so students usually stopped going to
school at age fourteen.

Source: *The Encyclopedia of New York City,* edited by Kenneth T.
Jackson, Yale University Press: New Haven & London; The
New York Historical Society: New York, 1995.

The Children's Aid Society is still active today, helping over 100,000 New York City children and their families each year. The Society's services include adoption and foster care, medical and dental care, counseling, preventive services, winter and summer camps, recreation, cultural enrichment, education and job training.

For more information, contact:

The Children's Aid Society
105 East 22nd Street
New York, NY 10010

About the Author

Joan Lowery Nixon is the acclaimed author of more than a hundred books for young readers. She has served as president of the Mystery Writers of America and as regional vice-president for the Southwest Chapter of that society. She is the only four-time winner of the Edgar Allan Poe Best Juvenile Mystery Award given by the Mystery Writers of America. She is also a two-time winner of the Golden Spur Award, which she won for *A Family Apart* and *In the Face of Danger,* the first and third books of the Orphan Train Adventures, which also include *Caught in the Act, A Place to Belong, A Dangerous Promise, Keeping Secrets,* and *Circle of Love.* She was moved by the true experiences of the children on the nineteenth-century orphan trains to research and write the Orphan Train Adventures, as well as the Orphan Train Children books, which include *Lucy's Wish* and *Will's Choice.*

Joan Lowery Nixon and her husband live in Houston.

Ink on Front cover 3-11-2 MB